10 Minute Tales

THOMAS & FRIENDS™

POP!
Goes
Thomas

Based on *The Railway Series* by the Rev. W. Awdry

When you see these symbols:

Read aloud
Read aloud to
your child.

Read alone
Support your child
as they read alone.

Read along
Read along with
your child.

EGMONT
We bring stories to life

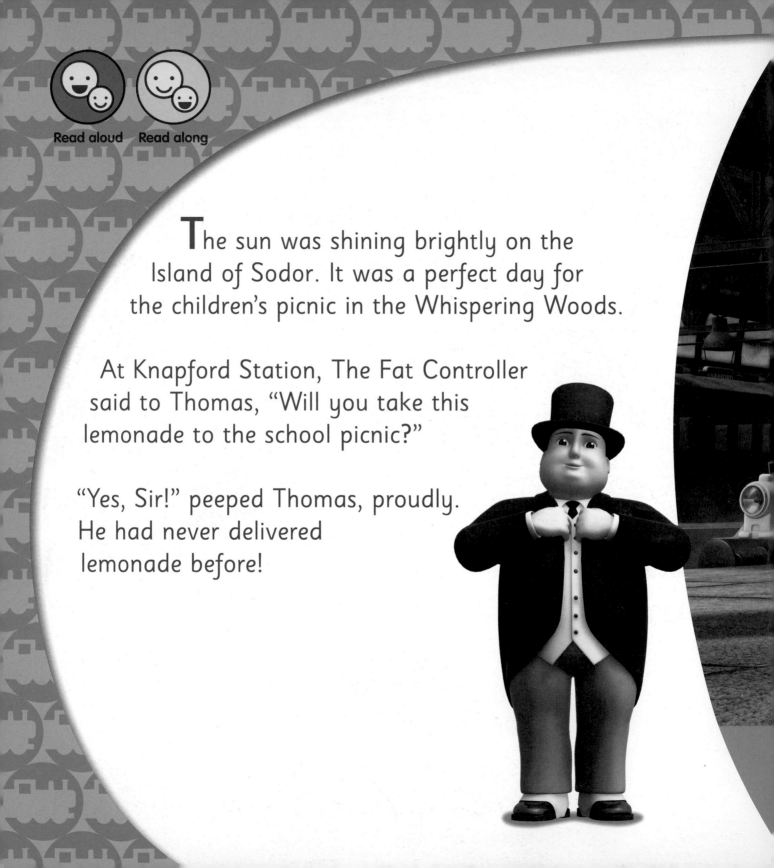

The sun was shining brightly on the Island of Sodor. It was a perfect day for the children's picnic in the Whispering Woods.

At Knapford Station, The Fat Controller said to Thomas, "Will you take this lemonade to the school picnic?"

"Yes, Sir!" peeped Thomas, proudly. He had never delivered lemonade before!

Read alone

Read aloud **Read along**

Thomas puffed out of the Station with his truck full of lemonade bottles. On the way to the Whispering Woods, Thomas went over some bumpy track.

"F-fizzling f-fireboxes!" he cried as he bounced over the bumps.

Rattle rattle, clink clink! went the bottles of lemonade in Thomas' truck.

Thomas goes over some bumpy track.
The lemonade bottles rattle and clink.

Read aloud Read along

Suddenly, Thomas heard a loud noise come from close behind him.

POP!

"Bust my buffers!" Thomas laughed. "That noise was very funny! Did it come from this bumpy track?"

He didn't know that the bumpy ride had made the cork pop out of a bottle, spilling the lemonade.

Read alone

POP! The bumps make a cork come out.
The lemonade spills, but Thomas doesn't know.

Soon, Thomas came to a junction.

"I can get to the Whispering Woods faster on the track straight ahead," he puffed. "But the left track is very bumpy. If I take it, I might hear that funny noise again!"

So Thomas steamed onto the bumpy track.

POP! POP! POP! The silly sounds were back!

Thomas goes on another bumpy track.
He hears the noise again. **POP! POP! POP!**

Read alone

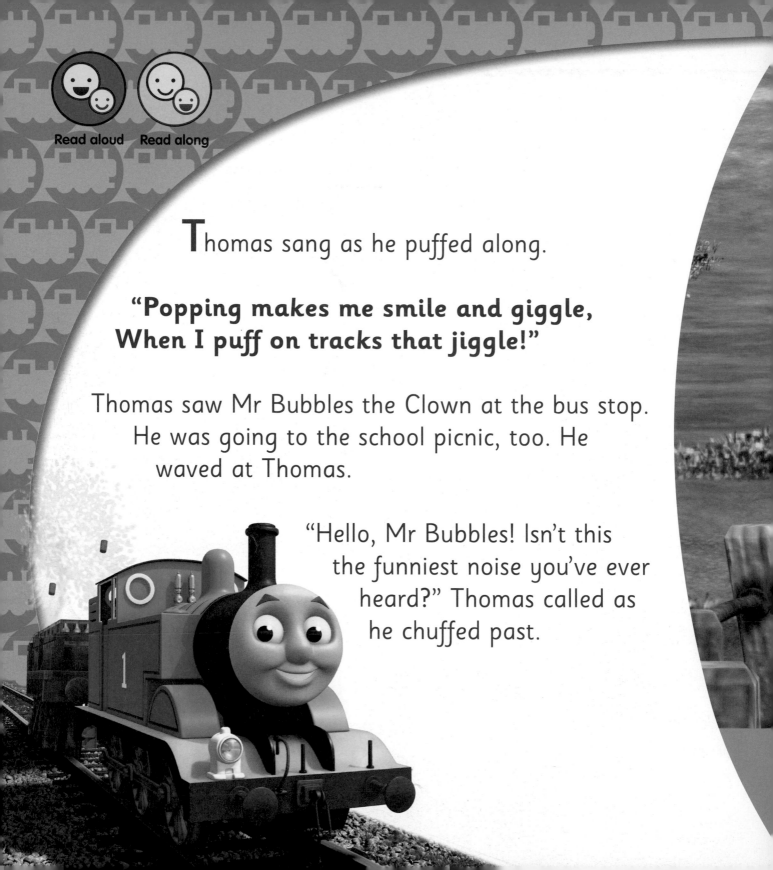

Read aloud   Read along

Thomas sang as he puffed along.

**"Popping makes me smile and giggle,
When I puff on tracks that jiggle!"**

Thomas saw Mr Bubbles the Clown at the bus stop.
He was going to the school picnic, too. He
waved at Thomas.

"Hello, Mr Bubbles! Isn't this
the funniest noise you've ever
heard?" Thomas called as
he chuffed past.

Read alone

Thomas passes Mr Bubbles the Clown.
He is going to the picnic, too.

Read aloud   Read along

In Thomas' truck, lots of corks were popping out of the lemonade bottles. **POP! POP! POP!**

One cork flew towards Mr Bubbles and knocked his red clown nose into a drain. Mr Bubbles was very upset!

But Thomas still didn't know about the popping corks. He puffed away cheerfully.

Read alone

POP! A cork flies towards Mr Bubbles.
It knocks his clown nose into a drain.

Read aloud   Read along

Thomas steamed down the bumpy track. Along the way, the lemonade bottles rattled and more corks popped out, spilling lemonade everywhere.

At the Bakery, Thomas saw the Bakers carefully putting boxes of cakes on the platform. Emily was coming to collect the cakes for the picnic.

The Bakers have made cakes for the picnic.
Emily is coming to collect them.

Read alone

POP! POP! POP!

"Isn't this the funniest noise you've ever heard?" Thomas laughed. As he puffed away, he didn't realise that the popping corks were flying right towards the Bakers!

"Oh! Ah!" cried the Bakers as they were hit by the corks. They were so surprised that they dropped the boxes. All the cakes fell onto the ground and were spoiled!

POP! The corks hit the Bakers.
They drop all the cakes on the ground!

Read alone

Read aloud   Read along

Near the Whispering Woods, Thomas stopped at a red signal. The bumpy track was causing more bottles to pop their corks and spill the lemonade.

POP! POP! POP!

As the Signalman went to change the light, a cork flew right into the signal box. The Signalman was so surprised that he pulled the wrong lever!

POP! Some corks fly into a signal box.
The Signalman pulls the wrong lever.

Read aloud   Read along

James was puffing along the track behind Thomas, carrying the children to the picnic.

Just then, his track changed because the Signalman had pulled the wrong lever. James was sent into a short siding, but he was going too fast to stop!

"Flatten my funnel!" he cried, closing his eyes tight.

BANG! James hit the buffers, but luckily, no one was hurt.

James is taking the children to the picnic. But the Signalman sends him on the wrong track!

When Thomas arrived at the Whispering Woods, The Fat Controller was waiting on the platform. He was very cross.

"Thomas, you have caused confusion and delay!" boomed The Fat Controller. "Mr Bubbles has lost his nose. The cakes are spoiled. James has bashed into the buffers. And the bottles in your truck have lost their corks. The lemonade is all gone!"

Before Thomas could answer, he heard a loud noise ...

The Fat Controller is cross.
Thomas has caused lots of trouble!

POP!

Suddenly, the very last cork popped out
of a lemonade bottle and sailed up in the air.
It flew towards The Fat Controller and knocked
his hat right off his head!

Thomas gasped. "Cinders and ashes! Those
funny popping noises were from the corks.
This is all my fault!" he wheeshed.

Thomas felt terrible. He had
ruined the picnic for
the children.

POP! The last cork flies up high. It knocks
The Fat Controller's hat right off his head!

Read aloud   Read along

Thomas had an idea. "I can put this right, Sir!" he puffed. But there wasn't much time. He pumped his pistons and raced back the way he had come.

First, he steamed to the Bakery. The Bakers gave him more cakes for the picnic. They loaded the boxes onto Thomas' truck.

Thomas wants to fix his mistakes.
He races to the Bakery for more cakes.

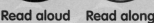

Next, Thomas sped to Knapford Station to get more lemonade. As he waited for the crates to be loaded, he saw Mr Bubbles on the platform.

"Look, Thomas. I bought a new red nose!" said Mr Bubbles.

"I'm sorry about the corks," peeped Thomas. "May I take you to the picnic?"

"What a splendid idea!" Mr Bubbles smiled.

Thomas gets Mr Bubbles and more lemonade from the Station. Mr Bubbles has a new nose!

Read aloud   Read along

Thomas puffed back to the Whispering Woods. He was very careful not to bump the bottles in his truck this time!

When he arrived at the picnic with the lemonade, cakes, and Mr Bubbles, the children clapped and cheered with delight.

"Well done, Thomas," smiled The Fat Controller. "You have saved the picnic."

Thomas was so happy to be Really Useful to the children, he whistled, "Peep! Peep!"

Read alone

The children cheer when Thomas arrives at the picnic. He is a Really Useful Engine, after all!